Dear Reader;

Mountains To Climb is my fourth children's story and is very special to me. Through the characters it describes the values, spirit and courage I have observed over the years in friends and family. To those mentioned below and to so many others whose inspiration and love have immeasurably enriched my life, I gratefully dedicate Mountains To Climb.

To: *Alicia, Cesar, Ivan, Fredy, Maria, Mauricio, Patricia ... my godchildren in South America.*

Bob, my brother, who courageously battled epilepsy every day of his life.

Nina O'brien, my mother-in-law, traveling companion who is 85 years young and is loved equally by all who know her in the U.S. and South America.

Marcus Clayton Thomas, friend and talented artist who is able to create beautiful paintings holding a paint brush between his teeth.

Marcy Scott, inspirational teacher who sees with her heart and hands.

Ed Stewart, advisor to a fortunate generation of high school young men.

Keewaydin: a camp whose democratic philosophy, uncompromising values and reverence for nature has enriched the lives of thousands of young people.

Jack Crompton, friend and talented illustrator who brings to life the spirit and love I hope my characters and stories convey.

Richard M. Wainwright

I dedicate the illustrations of this book to my dear sister Nancy, her husband Ed and their family. -J.S.C.

FAMILY LIFE
PUBLISHING

Published by Family Life Publishing
Dennis, Massachusetts 02638

Text Copyright © 1991 Richard M. Wainwright \ Illustrations Copyright © 1991 Jack Crompton

Book and Jacket Design by Crompton, Ltd., Cape Cod, Massachusetts
Printed in Singapore by Tien Wah Press \ Published in the United States of America 1991

Library of Congress Cataloging-in-Publication Data

Wainwright, Richard M.
Mountains To Climb

Summary: A young South American boy and his one-eyed llama travel to the United States and discover
that with perserverance social obstacles and physical handicaps can be overcome.
[1. Physically handicapped--Fiction. 2. Llamas--Fiction. 3. Prejudices--Fiction. 4. Friendship--Fiction.]
I. Crompton, Jack. ill. II. Mountains To Climb
PZ7 .W1317Mo 1991 [Fic]--dc20

ISBN 0-9619566-3-1

Mountains to Climb

Written by Richard M. Wainwright
Illustrated by Jack Crompton

To: *Jacob*

Remember: you too
can climb mountains
- One step at a time!

With best wishes
Richard M. Wainwright

From: Grandma with

1

love!

Best Wishes,
Richard M. Wainwright
1992

oberto's eyes were open but he remained snuggled beneath the thick alpaca blanket knowing his mother would soon call him for breakfast. It was cold. Mornings were always cold at 9,000 feet above sea level in South America's Andes mountains. Roberto lived in one of the adobe houses with orange-tiled roofs which dotted the terraced green slopes of the mountain. Five miles away nestled in the valley beside the river was the region's village with its stores, church, town hall and Roberto's school.

The combined smells of wood smoke and cooking food drifted through the house. Quinua, corn tortillas and coffee with milk would soon be ready. Roberto's father had left an hour before sun up to work in their fields preparing them for new crops of maize, potatoes and vegetables.

Although it was still dark, Roberto knew it was time to get up. The sun always took its time to climb above the mountain peaks and bring its warmth and light to the Andean valleys. Roberto quickly dressed and rolled up his straw sleeping mat. Roberto's family worked hard and Roberto worked hard too. He had several chores to do before breakfast. He whistled a happy tune as he fed the pigs and chickens. After collecting eggs he had to take the family's five llamas to a nearby field to graze.

The llamas were used to carry seed to the fields and later in the year carry crops to market. Their fine wool was woven into ponchos, blankets and sweaters.

3

Roberto loved all the animals, especially the llamas. He hurried to the stable. He hoped this would be the day. His mother and father had promised him that the next baby llama would be his and Blanca was expecting. As he entered the stable he knew something had happened. The three other female llamas had formed a circle around Blanca. Almost completely hidden from view were four tiny, wobbly brown legs. All the llamas knew Roberto and were not afraid as he approached. Reaching up to gently pat Blanca's neck, Roberto slowly walked around Blanca to take a close look at her baby.

Roberto smiled. His baby llama shyly had its head tucked into Blanca's side. He could see it was a female, tan with a white diamond on its forehead. She looked perfect and then turned to peek at Roberto. Roberto stared in shock. The little llama had only one eye. He couldn't believe it. She was beautiful but  she had only one eye. The little llama took a hesitant step toward Roberto and nuzzled her head into Roberto's hand which hung by his side. Her touch made his surprise and shock pass away. Slowly he sank to his knees and gently hugged the little llama.

"Your name will be Consuelo," he whispered, "and I will take good care of you."

"Hola, Roberto, buenos días, how are you today and how is Blanca doing ?"

"Buenos días Father," Roberto replied, "I'm fine and thanks to Blanca we now have six llamas."

"That's wonderful!" Roberto's mother and father exclaimed. " Tell us about your llamita ... is it a male or female ?"

"Well ...," began Roberto, "She's light brown with pretty white patches ... she's really beautiful. I love her and named her Consuelo, but ..."

"But what ?" his father asked.

"Consuelo has only one eye," Roberto whispered.

"Only one eye," his mother and father gasped, "are you sure?"

"Yes, I am sure," Roberto replied " but it doesn't matter. She is gentle and affectionate. I will take good care of her."

Roberto's parents smiled. They would have tried to sell the llama if Roberto had not wanted to keep her but they were very pleased with his decision.

Each morning after completing his chores, Roberto would brush and talk to Consuelo before leaving for school. Later when he returned, he had only to whistle and Consuelo would come running across the fields knowing Roberto would pat her and maybe even have a sweet carrot.

Consuelo grew fast. In six months she was more than half the size of her mother. Everyday she would follow Blanca to the fields. Since it was harvest time, Roberto's father had been picking the corn and having the llamas carry the full sacks back to the house.

"Would you like to go to the market with us Saturday?" Roberto's father asked at supper one evening. "Consuelo could carry two small sacks of corn."

Roberto nodded enthusiastically. This would be Consuelo's first trip to the village. He would be proud to take her. Roberto thought she was the most beautiful and gentlest little llama in the world. He had long ago forgotten she was different than other llamas.

Roberto's father tenderly shook his son. It was three o'clock in the morning. The Saturday market began at sunrise and it took over two hours to lead the llamas down the steep path to the main trail to the village.

The moon slowly disappeared from the night sky. Soon the rosy glow of dawn chased away the dark, silhouetting the towering mountain peaks. Roberto's mother and father led the adult llamas and Roberto followed with Consuelo. They met other families with laden llamas as they entered the main trail. Roberto kept a tight grasp on Consuelo's rope. As they neared the village hundreds of people converged on the market place. It was still cold so the men wore their blue wool ponchos and the women long dark skirts and warm shawls.

Roberto could see many types of vegetables being carried to the market not only on llamas but also on men's and women's backs. Hundreds of other things from all over the world were arriving by trucks which had made the long trip from the city.

It was always a wonderful and exciting sight. People everywhere stood behind tables or sat on the ground selling everything from carrots to cameras. Handmade ceramic bowls, straw baskets, rope, metal pots and pans, radios, clothes from factories...you only had to look to find what you needed.

One section of the market was set aside for animals. It was easy to find as the sounds of cackling chickens, quacking ducks, squealing pigs, the lowing of cows and the braying of donkeys filled the air.

Another area contained the sidewalk restaurants selling all types of food. Vendors with small portable stoves shouted the names of the dishes that were steaming in their pots. Salchichas, huevos con arroz, sopa de chivo and many more typical foods. Delicious aromas reminded Roberto that they hadn't eaten any breakfast. He knew after they sold the corn there would be plenty of time to eat and explore the market.

Through the ever moving crowd and honking horns Roberto and his parents slowly made their way toward the large trucks that were waiting to buy vegetables to take back to the city.

One of the drivers spotted Roberto's father. "Hola amigo," he shouted. "Let me see your corn. I'm paying the best price."

Roberto's father stopped and smiled. All the truck drivers said that. Roberto's mother held the rope of the lead llama while her husband talked with several men before agreeing to a price and shaking hands with one of the truck drivers. It took only a few moments to unload the sacks of corn. Now the family would have time for breakfast and shopping.

After they all had a big breakfast of rice, eggs, meat, bread and milk, Roberto's mother left to buy sugar, flour, beans and some cloth for new shirts for Roberto and his father. Roberto and his father led the llamas to the edge of the market. "Please watch the llamas, Roberto," his father asked. "I need to buy some nails, seed corn and potatoes."

"Of course, Father," Roberto replied.

His father smiled and gave his son a pat on the back before disappearing in the crowd. Roberto stood beside Consuelo gently stroking her head. Several much bigger boys wandered by. One stopped and stared at Consuelo. "Hey guys," he called to his friends, "come on back. Look! A one-eyed llama. What a freak."

The other boys crowded around Roberto and Consuelo pointing at the little llama and laughing.

"His family's so poor he can't afford a normal llama," one of the boys jeered. "Hey kid, why don't you sell your llama to the circus and buy some new clothes?"

Roberto moved in front of Consuelo trying to protect her from the taunts of the boys. He didn't say anything but he clenched his fists. He wasn't scared and the look on his face told the older boys that they had made Roberto angry. They had had their fun so they decided to move along laughing, pointing and covering one of their eyes.

Roberto, now alone, remained angry and also sad. A single tear slowly slid down Roberto's cheek. The mean words and insults of the boys of course had not bothered Consuelo, but they had hurt Roberto. He loved Consuelo. Her gentle, affectionate nature and willingness to do everything she could, made her perfect in Roberto's eyes. She deserved everyone's respect. As far as Roberto was concerned she was better than normal.

Soon Roberto's mother and father returned with all their purchases. His father had brought Roberto his favorite fruit - mangos, which were grown near the coast, and a quimbolito - a sweet corn pastry. Roberto thanked his parents - he wasn't hungry and would save them for later. In a few moments everything was packed. Roberto's father took the lead rope of the first llama and they began their long walk home up the mountain.

Roberto was quiet on the way home and sat silently at supper.

"What's the matter, Son ?" his father asked.

Roberto looked up from his plate and told his parents about the boys who had ridiculed Consuelo. When he was finished his father spoke again.

"Sadly," he began, "there are people in this world that judge humans and animals by appearance. These people think physical looks, skin color, size and even clothes are most important. They do not look for qualities that are really desirable such as honesty, courage, gentleness and the willingness to work hard. Roberto, your mother and I have always been proud of you because you understand what qualities are truly important. Your life will be happier and fuller because you do. Someday you will have the opportunity to share these beliefs with others. You may not change the way of thinking of everyone you meet but some will listen and will become more tolerant of differences that exist in our world."

Roberto smiled. He knew what his father said was right and true. He simply had needed to hear it again, and he went to bed feeling at peace.

Days and months flew quickly by. Early morning chores, the daily long walks to school, homework, planting and harvesting in the fields with his parents, and camping trips in the mountains with his father and friends filled Roberto's life to the fullest. Of course, not a day went by without a visit and talk with Consuelo.

One Saturday began as usual with a trip to the market. After selling their vegetables, Roberto's father stopped in the Correo (Post Office) to see if they had any mail. Much to his delight, he found a letter from his brother who had moved to the United States. The brothers were close and often wrote each other. Roberto's father tucked the letter inside his shirt and looked forward to sharing it with his wife and son at supper.

After completing the meal, Roberto's father took out the letter and read it out loud. His brother wrote that they were happy in the United States although they missed the beautiful Andes Mountains, friends and family. He had a good job and a nice house with almost an acre of land.

Roberto's father paused and a sad-happy expression came over his face as he continued to read the letter ... "we would love to have Roberto come to the United States and live with us for a year or two. He would go to school, learn English, and he could even bring Consuelo. We can arrange for his tickets if you would like to have him come."

No one said anything. Roberto's mother and father looked at their son. Finally his mother said, " We would miss you terribly Roberto, but it would be a wonderful opportunity. What do you think ?"

Roberto couldn't answer right away. The United States had always been a distant land far beyond the mountains. It was one of those far off countries that was often discussed in his geography class but to actually go there was something he never imagined even in his dreams.

Roberto had always been fond of his aunt and uncle. It wouldn't be like living with strangers. Roberto raised his eyes. " I will miss you, too," he began. "It will be a new world for me and learning English will help me enter the University some day." Roberto smiled. "Yes, I would like to go and I think Consuelo would like to go, too." Roberto got up from the table and hugged his mother and father for a long time.

Three months passed. Roberto would leave for the United States tomorrow. He couldn't sleep and quietly got out of bed tip-toeing to the front door. He sat down on the bench outside and leaned back against the adobe wall of the house. He watched the full moon inch its way above the mountain tops. Of all stars and constellations in the sky the Southern Cross was his favorite and it sparkled brilliantly in the clear night sky.

A few moments later his father silently appeared and sat down next to Roberto. "Excited ?", he asked.

"Yes," Roberto replied, "and scared, too. I will miss you, Mother, my friends and our mountains. Maybe there will be things in North America I will not be able to do. The language and their customs may be too difficult for me."

Roberto's father did not answer right away. When he spoke he asked, " Remember when we went on our first camping trip and decided to climb to the top of Pinchincha. You thought it was too high, too difficult but we reached the summit. How ?"

Roberto smiled. It had been a lesson he usually remembered but tonight had forgotten. "We climbed it one step at a time," he quietly replied.

" Remember, Roberto," his father continued, "In every person's life there will be many mountains to climb ... some harder than others but most conquerable ... *one step at a time.*"

The moon disappeared below the snow-covered mountain peaks. In a few hours Roberto would leave. He was no longer worried ... he would remember his father's words.

The following morning, Roberto and his parents headed down the trail to the village. Roberto led Consuelo who carried two suitcases. At the end of the path a family friend, Jose Cisneros, waited with a truck which would take Roberto and Consuelo to the port on the coast. Roberto had a ticket on a freighter for himself and Consuelo. Everything had been arranged.

After Consuelo was loaded into the back of the truck, Roberto hugged his parents. He climbed up next to Mr. Cisneros who started the truck. Soon Roberto's waving parents disappeared from view.

Five hours later Roberto stood on a dock looking up at a gigantic freighter. Everywhere men were busy putting cargo of all types into big nets which were lifted on board by huge cranes. Roberto helped position the wooden planks for Consuelo who carefully descended from the truck. All the activity and noise made her a little nervous and she began to hum (as all llamas do when they are worried). As the truck driver placed Roberto's suitcases on the ground, a large man with a black beard approached.

"Welcome, Roberto!" he called with a big smile. "We have been expecting you and Consuelo. I'm Captain Chavez and my ship will be taking you to the United States."

Roberto shook the Captain's hand and introduced Mr. Cisneros.

"We will get underway soon ... time to get on board," Captain Chavez continued. "We have a place on deck especially for Consuelo." He paused noticing that she had only one eye but he didn't say anything. "Your cabin is next to mine. You lead Consuelo and I'll carry the suitcases."

Roberto shook hands with Mr.Cisneros who patted him on the back and wished him a safe journey. The gangplank was empty ... a few steps and they were aboard.

Behind the cabins and the wheelhouse the sailors had built a pen with a wooden floor and a leanto for Consuelo. There was a box of hay and a large dish of water attached to the lean-to so it would not slide around. Roberto led

" Roberto, I hope you and Consuelo will have a wonderful time in the United States. You both would make fine sailors so if you ever decide to make your home at sea instead of in the mountains, let me know. We were happy to have you aboard."

Roberto had a big grin on his face as he shook the Captain's hand and thanked him for everything. It was a voyage he knew that he would never forget. He turned and waved as he slowly led Consuelo down the gangplank.

After big hugs from his aunt and uncle, Roberto led Consuelo up and into his uncle's pick-up truck.

"Vamonos a casa," said Roberto's uncle. "Let's go home," he repeated in English.

Roberto sat between his aunt and uncle staring at the huge office and apartment buildings that appeared to almost touch the clouds.

"What do you think of our skyscrapers?" Roberto's aunt asked in Spanish as they drove through the city.

"They may be taller than some of our mountains," Roberto replied laughing. His aunt and uncle laughed too.

It took almost an hour to slowly wind their way out of the great city. Roberto asked questions about everything new he saw. Finally they turned onto a super highway and headed north. Five hours away was the town where Roberto's aunt and uncle lived.

Following Roberto's one hundreth question in Spanish, his uncle said: "Roberto, now is the time for you to begin learning English. Your school will begin in less than two months and you must be able to understand your teachers. When you want to ask a question, 'Que es eso?' is translated, 'what is that?' "

Roberto repeated, " What is that?" pointing to a house they were passing.

"That is a house," his aunt replied, "esa es una casa."

"A house," repeated Roberto.

The next few hours flew by as Roberto began asking questions in English and repeating the English answers. Seeing something and hearing what it was called at the same time seemed to make it easier to remember. Roberto's English vocabulary grew rapidly. In a restaurant Roberto added an English - French term " pie a la mode." As he finished the last delicious bit of pie he knew he would never forget "pie à la mode."

The sun was setting as Roberto's uncle drove into his driveway. Roberto's aunt and uncle's home looked very different from his home in South America. It was all brick with black asphalt shingles covering the roof. A screened-in porch connected the house and the garage. It looked very nice.

conversation in the house was in English. After the family's evening meal together Roberto would watch television and that helped his English, too.

The first day of school was surprisingly cold for September. Roberto put on his favorite poncho and bright wool hat with ear flaps. It was only a few minutes walk to the school bus stop at the end of the street.

Soon a big yellow bus came to a stop in front of Roberto. Its door swung open and he climbed aboard. "Good morning," said the lady bus driver with a smile.

"Good morning," replied Roberto before walking down the aisle of the almost full bus. Some of the young people laughed as Roberto walked by. Others pointed at him as he passed and turned around to watch him. Roberto took an empty seat. He remembered the day at the market when the boys taunted Consuelo and made fun of his clothes. As the children continued to stare Roberto felt very much alone.

The ride to the school took only a few minutes. When the bus stopped all the students rushed out of the bus. A teacher at the school's entrance greeted Roberto and directed him to his homeroom. As he walked along the corridor he was aware that other students were stopping to point him out ... some laughed, others just shook their heads.

Roberto received his class schedule and at the sound of a bell went to a different classroom. He was given books for math, science, history, English and geography. The final bell rang at 2:15 P.M. and all the students headed for the waiting buses. Although many students had obviously noticed Roberto, most had simply laughed or stared. Not one student had spoken to him.

Roberto was sad and puzzled. He had many school friends in South America. He had hoped he would make many friends in the United States. Maybe people were different in this country. Discouraged, he walked into his aunt and uncle's home, changed his clothes and went to care for Consuelo.

The first school week went by quickly. Roberto could understand most of what his teachers said but found the written homework very difficult. His aunt and uncle helped him every night. He mentioned that the students acted as if he simply didn't exist. Each student seemed to be a member of a group of friends which went from one class to another.

On Roberto's fifth day in his English class the teacher read the list of the week's vocabulary words. The students were asked to define the word the teacher wrote on the blackboard. One of the week's words was "discrimination." One student raised her hand and defined the word by saying, "Discrimination is judging people by their religion."

Next a boy stood up and said, " Discrimination is not treating people equally because their parents are rich or poor."

Roberto had discussed all the words with his aunt and uncle. He remembered his father's words about the challenges he would face in the United States. Maybe this was the time to take the first step to climb the mountain. He felt alone, sad, and a little angry. He raised his hand.

"Yes, Roberto," the teacher said, recognizing him. "Please stand."

Roberto slowly stood facing the class. In a quiet but strong voice he began, " Six weeks ago, I come to your country from South America. I am sorry I not speak good English, but I try. Some of my clothes are different, my face is different and color different. I am new. No one speaks to me. I know I can learn much from you and want to know the customs of your beautiful country. I hope also that maybe there are some things you would like to know about my country and our people. We are different, that is good. But much the same and that is good, too. Thank you."

Roberto's classmates at first were silent. One by one they began to smile and clap loudly. "Bravo," said Roberto's teacher. "I am sorry I do not speak Spanish. It is a beautiful language. Roberto your English is fine and will improve rapidly and your ideas speak eloquently. Thank you for having the courage to share your feelings with us."

A bell rang signaling the end of the class. As Roberto gathered up his books he felt a hand on his shoulder.

At the beginning of the trail, the six boys and Mr. Stewart, the club's advisor, greeted Roberto who had led Consuelo from his aunt and uncle's home. Consuelo had on her new halter and her bells quietly tinkled as she walked. Roberto carried a backpack and Consuelo carried empty saddle boxes. When Roberto announced that Consuelo could easily carry the tents and cooking equipment she became an instant hero. Usually the boys had to divide this equipment up and carry it along with their own clothes, sleeping bag and food. Roberto stood beside Consuelo as each boy and Mr. Stewart slowly approached and petted her. She smelled each hand and soon Consuelo accepted all the new smells and noise of the group.

Clouds were gradually filling the sky as they moved out in high spirits. For the American boys it was exciting to be back-packing with a llama. For Roberto it was like being home. At first the trail was wide and flat, but after an hour it became narrow and zig-zagged steeply. Mr. Stewart led and Roberto and Consuelo brought up the rear. It was a difficult climb to the treeline. Difficult for everyone except Consuelo and Roberto who were accustomed to many hours of climbing each day.

Leaving the trees below they began to follow the rocky ridge which would take them to Eagles Nest Lookout where they hoped to camp for the night. The ridge offered little protection. Roberto was concerned as he watched the white clouds changing to a threatening gray. The smell of heavy rain and strong winds was in the air. Just before four o'clock they reached their goal. The view of the valley far below was beautiful but a few large raindrops and a steady breeze made setting up camp more important than enjoying the vista.

Noting the direction of the wind, Roberto knew finding a protected spot for the tents was the task of the moment. The Andes above the treeline was very similar and he spoke to Mr. Stewart before leaving the group. In less than five minutes he returned. He had found an almost hidden entrance to a small flat area which was protected by large overhang and several huge boulders.

" Perfect", said Mr. Stewart as everyone filed through the narrow opening. "We can put our tents under the ledge and the boulders in front will deflect most of the wind."

The next hour was a race against the elements. The tents were quickly erected and tied down. The cooking equipment and food were unpacked and placed under the overhang. Roberto tethered Consuelo in a sheltered spot. She was not concerned, as the weather in the Andes often brought cold temperatures, wind, rain and even snow. Her warm wool coat was more than enough to protect her in these mountains.

Mr. Stewart, Doug and Craig lit the kerosene stove and in a few minutes a beef stew was bubbling. All the boys were starved and as each filled their plates the rain and wind began in earnest so everyone scurried into the tents to eat. It was a real downpour with strong gusts of wind. Mr. Stewart was thankful Roberto had found this protected spot.

Dry and warm in the tents the boys talked of other trips and asked Roberto about his experiences in the Andes with his father. The wind whistled and howled for a while. Roberto put on his poncho and once more checked Consuelo and the tent ropes. Both were fine.

Roberto reached into his backpack and brought out his *quena* and began to play it. Everyone stopped talking to listen to the beautiful music Roberto was making on the cane flute. Each note had a beauty of its own as it pierced the silence of the night and echoed across the mountain top. The lovely music created a magical never-to-be-forgotten moment for his friends.

"Bravo! Bravo!" shouted everyone when Roberto stopped, and the applause drifted away into the night.

"That was my favorite," explained Roberto. "*El Condor Pasa*. It is a song about the majestic condor which lives in our Andes ... it is the symbol of the mountains all South Americans love." After a few more songs and some cookies it was time to crawl into the sleeping bags. Now a gentle rain and whispering wind made the music for sleep.

Morning came slowly to the mountains. A gray mist still enveloped the tents. Roberto, Keith and Mr. Stewart made breakfast as the others packed their gear and struck the tents. After the boys had a hearty breakfast of boiled eggs, bread, jelly and cocoa,the cooking equipment was packed in one of Consuelo's boxes. The rocky ground was still wet from the night's rain. It would be a slippery descent. In single file the group started back down the trail.

Not far from the treeline the path narrowed. Loose, wet stones littered the trail. Mr. Stewart cautiously moved forward. He placed his left foot on what he thought was a secure flat rock. The next instant he felt himself flying through the air and then tumbling over the edge of the trail and falling ten feet to a wide rock ledge. Pain shot through his legs and ankles as he hit the ledge. He crumpled into a heap.

Mark, who had been next in line, watched in horror as Mr. Stewart disappeared over the edge. He froze and shouted to the others what had happened and warned them to come very carefully. The boys crawled to the edge of the trail and called to Mr. Stewart. It seemed forever before Mr. Stewart spoke. "Most of me is all right," he announced, slowly sitting up and unbuckling his backpack. "But I'm afraid my ankles are at least sprained. I can't walk."

Roberto had taken off his backpack. Opening it he began to take out several leather ropes. " These are tumplines," he explained. "They are very strong and we use them all the time in the Andes to carry heavy loads and if necessary to make stretchers. Doug, can you and Mark find us two straight saplings we can use for the poles of a stretcher? Craig, Keith, Lonny and I with Consuelo's help will pull Mr. Stewart up."

Roberto quickly tied several of the leather ropes together. He then found a secure place where he could sit and firmly brace his legs. Lonny tied one end of the rope around his waist and Roberto secured the other end around his.

" Ready!" Roberto said as Lonny slowly lowered himself over the rim of the trail looking for foot and handholds that would allow him to climb down to Mr. Stewart. Roberto took up the slack ready to hold tight if Lonny slipped.

A few minutes later Lonny was kneeling next to Mr. Stewart. He untied the rope and fastened it to Mr. Stewart's pack. Roberto and Craig quickly pulled it up to the trail. Down came the leather rope again. This time Lonny tied it around Mr. Stewart.

Roberto brought Consuelo near. He tied his end of the rope around her chest and held her bridle. "Ready?" Roberto called. "Ready," replied Mr. Stewart. Roberto led Consuelo up the trail. The leather rope tightened. Lonny helped Mr. Stewart as Consuelo and the boys slowly pulled him upward. Mr. Stewart used his arms and knees. Any weight on his feet caused terrible pain. Finally his hands felt the edge of the trail and he pulled himself over the top. He knew he never would have made it up without the boys and Consuelo.

Soon Doug and Mark returned with two strong eight foot poles. Roberto used the tumplines to weave a leather stretcher. In a short time it was ready for Mr. Stewart. Doug, Lonny, Keith and Craig picked up the four ends of the poles. It would be slow going but the boys were able to carry Mr Stewart. Roberto tied Mr. Stewart's pack on top of his. It was a heavy load but with the tumpline across his fore-head he knew he had carried as much in the Andes. Roberto and Consuelo led the way warning those behind of loose and slippery rocks. It took hours for Roberto and the boys carrying Mr. Stewart to inch their way down the mountain.

When the trail leveled out, Mark went on ahead. He went right to Roberto's aunt and uncle's home. Mrs. Stewart was called first and then the parents of the other boys. By the time Mark and Roberto's aunt and uncle got to the trail, Mrs. Stewart and several of the boys' parents were waiting.

Roberto stood near Marcus who was leaning on his arm crutches. Roberto would carry most of Marcus's equipment and Consuelo would carry his sleeping bag as well as the tents and cooking equipment.

"Ready, Marcus?" Roberto asked. "Remember, we'll take our time. Consuelo and I will walk with you. Rest when you need to. There's no hurry. Loon Lake isn't going anywhere." Marcus smiled and nodded.

Mr. Stewart set a slow pace and the group stopped frequently. " You can't imagine how wonderful it is to be in the mountains," Keller commented to Lonny. "The smell of the pines, hearing the songs of the birds and even an occasional branch in the face is terrific," and he laughed.

Lonny answered, "Sorry about that branch ... being *your* eyes really takes concentration. It's easy to forget that my body automatically reacts to what my eyes see. Am I doing better? During the last half hour you haven't tripped over a rock or been whacked by a branch that I failed to mention."

Keller laughed again, " Keep improving, Lonny, and you'll get my seeing-eye dog award for the trip." Lonny barked loudly and both boys had to stop because they were laughing so hard.

By lunchtime, they had made it to the base of the steep hill that stood between the group and Loon Lake. This was one of Roberto's favorite spots. A rushing mountain stream cut though the sunny glen which was filled with beautiful wildflowers. Marcus and Roberto shared a large boulder and slowly ate their sandwiches.

"We're missing one knife and two forks," said Keller. Doug reached into the dishpan again and came up with one knife and two forks. "How did you know that, Keller?" he asked.

Keller smiled, "It's not really hard. People who are blind must be organized. Sometimes I count the steps from one room to another, from one classroom to another in school and even the number of steps to the street corner from the exit door. Counting forks and knives is really easy."

"I understand," said Keith, "but how do you know how much money you have when you go shopping?"

" That's not hard either," replied Keller. "One dollar bills are folded a particular way. If I am lucky enough to have a five, ten or twenty then I fold each one differently. I only need to know what denomination the bill is when I receive it."

Later that evening everyone gathered around the campfire. Roberto was asked to play his quena. He went to a tent and returned with his flute and with a guitar too.   "You may have thought this guitar was mine," he began, " since it was carried by Consuelo, but it isn't." Roberto walked over to Keller and gently placed it in his hands. "We have a little surprise for you."

Keller not only played the guitar very well but sang beautifully. He and Roberto had practiced a number of songs together and Keller had even learned the words in Spanish of two of Roberto's favorites. The quiet strumming of the guitar, the haunting notes of the quena and the flickering light of the campfire created a never to be forgotten ending of a perfect day.

Lying in his sleeping bag and looking up, Roberto could see that the Big Dipper in the northern sky shone as brightly as the Southern Cross. A loon's mournful cry echoed across the lake. Its melancholy call reminded Roberto he soon would be going home.

Roberto did not spend his last night alone in the United States. All the explorers came to Roberto's aunt and uncle's home. After everyone had arrived Roberto's aunt brought out a large cake and his uncle dished out huge scoops of ice cream. As the cake and ice cream disappeared the boys talked about all the fun times they had had during the past two years.

It was getting late when Keller and Lonny stood and asked for quiet. "Roberto," Lonny began, holding a large framed photograph, "we would like you to have this picture of all of us taken at Loon Lake. We hope it will always remind you of your friends in the U.S."

Keller also held a frame which contained a beautiful watercolor sketch of mountains with a llama in the foreground. Below the painting were several neatly printed sentences.

"Roberto, we hope you will also find a place for this gift in your home. Marcus painted the lovely picture and printed the words I wrote. This is what it says.

Roberto. Our friend from South America.

A Climber of Mountains
Who Sees With His Heart

We will miss you and Consuelo but we will never forget your friendship, leadership and ideas.
Lonny, Keith, Mark, Doug, Craig, Marcus, Keller and Mr. Stewart.